D0603634

For Jess xxx —C. H.

For Les —E. U.

BLOOMSBURY CHILDREN'S BOOKS
Bloomsbury Publishing Inc., part of Bloomsbury Publishing Plc
1385 Broadway, New York, NY 10018

BLOOMSBURY, BLOOMSBURY CHILDREN'S BOOKS, and the Diana logo
are trademarks of Bloomsbury Publishing Plc

First published in Great Britain in August 2018 by Bloomsbury Publishing Plc
Published in the United States of America in July 2019
by Bloomsbury Children's Books

Text copyright © 2018 by Caryl Hart
Illustrations copyright © 2018 by Edward Underwood

All rights reserved. No part of this publication may be reproduced or transmitted in any form or by any means, electronic or mechanical, including photocopying, recording, or any information storage or retrieval system, without prior permission in writing from the publisher.

Bloomsbury books may be purchased for business or promotional use. For information on bulk purchases please contact Macmillan Corporate and Premium Sales Department at specialmarkets@macmillan.com

Library of Congress Cataloging-in-Publication Data
Names: Hart, Caryl, author. | Underwood, Edward (Illustrator), illustrator.
Title: One shoe two shoes / by Caryl Hart ; illustrated by Edward Underwood.
Description: New York : Bloomsbury, 2019.
Summary: Introduces colors and the numbers one to ten as increasing
numbers of mice explore a wide variety of shoes.
Identifiers: LCCN 2018045842 (print) • LCCN 2018051389 (e-book)
ISBN 978-1-5476-0094-6 (hardcover) • ISBN 978-1-5476-0095-3 (e-book) • ISBN 978-1-5476-0096-0 (e-PDF)
Subjects: | CYAC: Shoes—Fiction. | Mice—Fiction. | Color—Fiction. | Counting—Fiction.
Classification: LCC PZ7.H25633 One 2019 (print) | LCC PZ7.H25633 (e-book) | DDC [E]—dc23
LC record available at https://lccn.loc.gov/2018045842

Art created with pencil, ink, and computer-assisted collage
Typeset in Filosofia
Book design by Goldy Broad
Printed in China by Leo Paper Products, Heshan, Guangdong
2 4 6 8 10 9 7 5 3 1

All papers used by Bloomsbury Publishing Plc are natural, recyclable products
made from wood grown in well-managed forests. The manufacturing processes
conform to the environmental regulations of the country of origin.

To find out more about our authors and books visit www.bloomsbury.com and sign up for our newsletters.

One Shoe Two Shoes

Caryl Hart

illustrated by

Edward Underwood

BLOOMSBURY
CHILDREN'S BOOKS
NEW YORK LONDON OXFORD NEW DELHI SYDNEY

One shoe

Two shoes

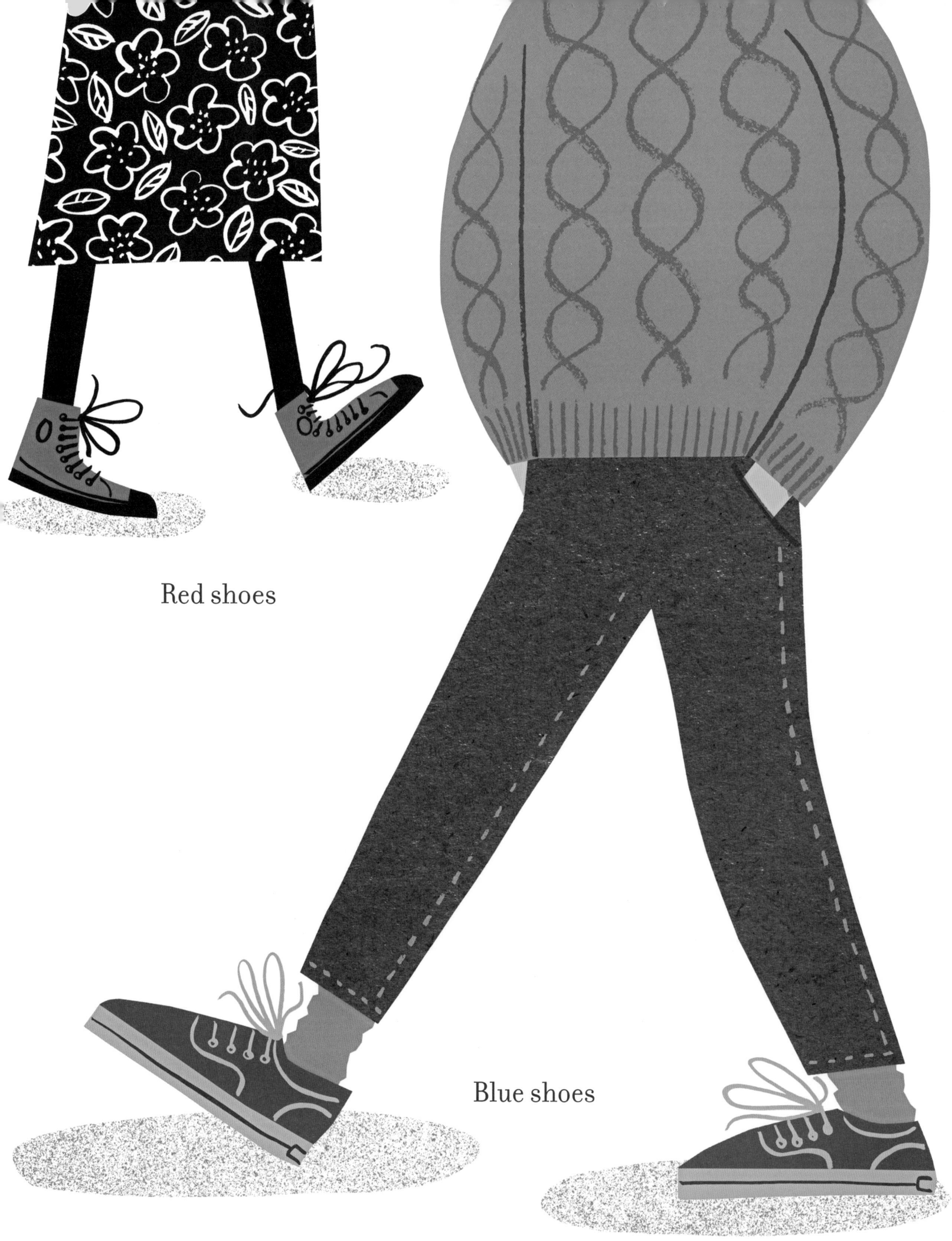
Red shoes
Blue shoes

Old shoes
New shoes

On their way to school shoes

Long laces tied in knots

Green pumps
with yellow spots

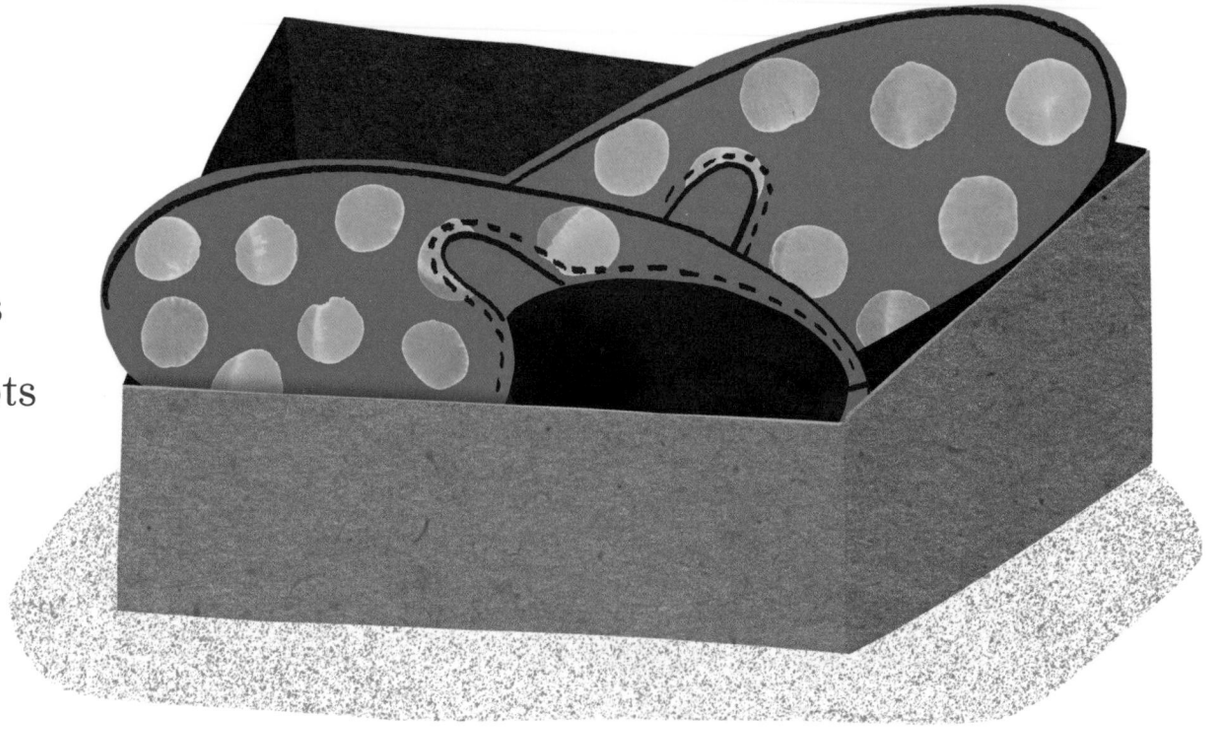

Party shoes

Artsy shoes
Cowboy boots
Flip-flops!

Two shoes make a pair.

Who's that hiding there?

Little mouse one

and little mouse two!

They've made a house

in someone's shoe!

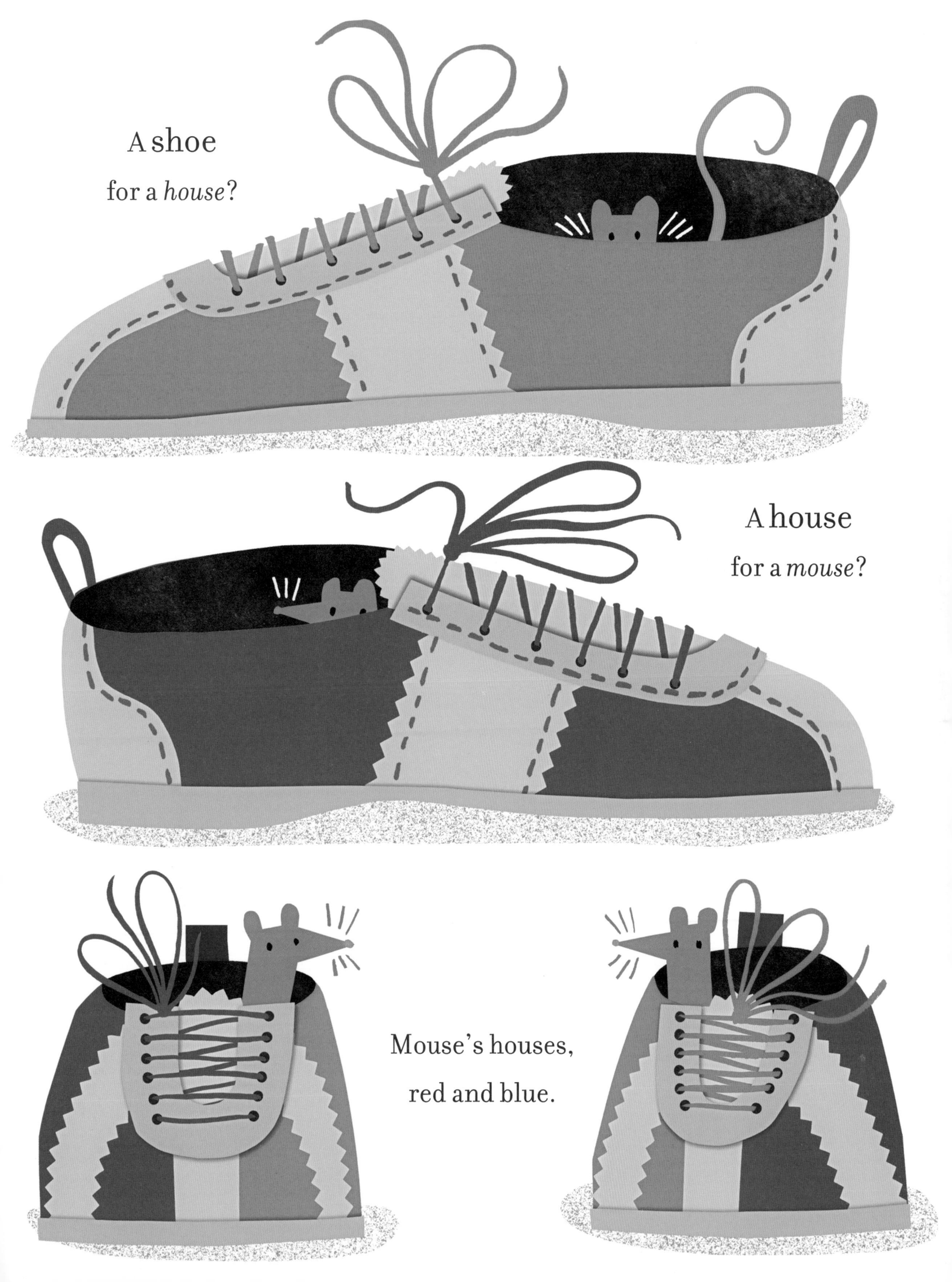
A shoe
for a *house*?
A house
for a *mouse*?
Mouse's houses,
red and blue.

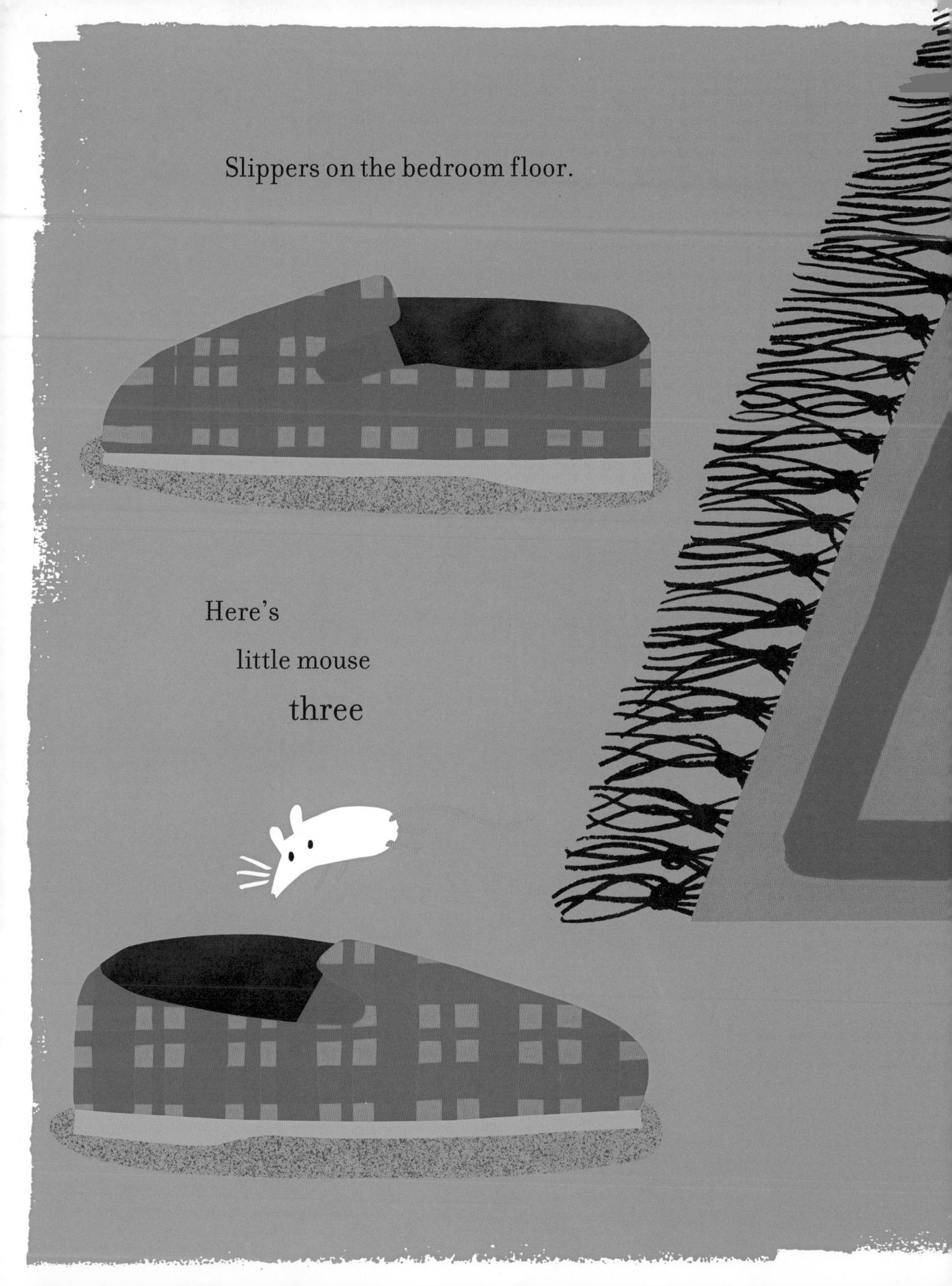

Slippers on the bedroom floor.

Here's

little mouse

three

and little mouse four!

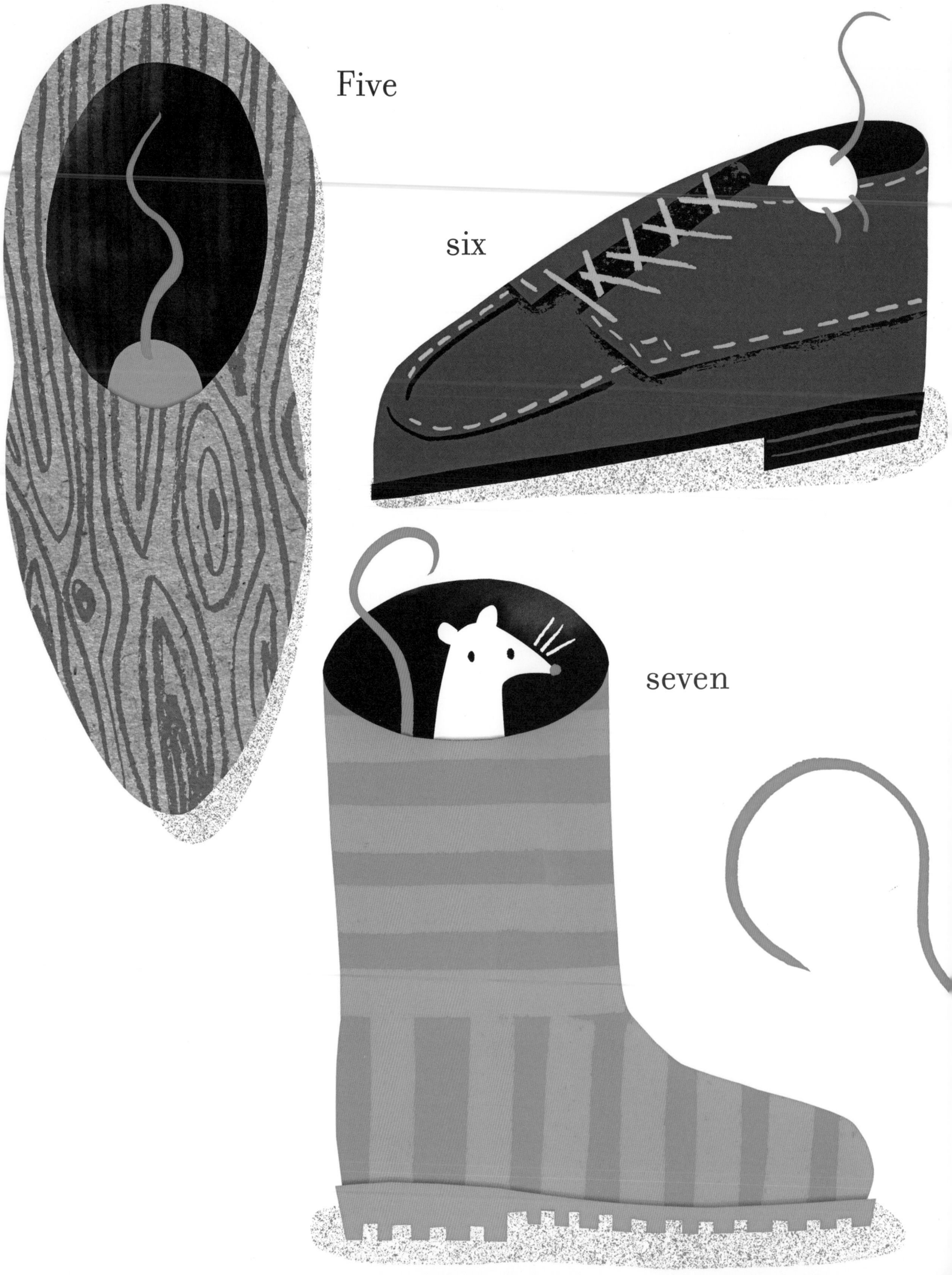
Five
six
seven

eight and nine

ten little white mice

all in line!

Pitter
Patter

Sniff

Lick

Doggy stretch
Good boy—
fetch!

Bounce away

Time to play

Hooray!